LOST IN TOKYO
Found in You

LOST IN TOKYO FOUND IN YOU

First edition. December 24, 2024.

Copyright © 2024 Sibusiso Anthon Mkhwanazi.

ISBN: 979-8230836698

Written by Sibusiso Anthon Mkhwanazi.

Also by Sibusiso Anthon Mkhwanazi

Million-Dollar Decade

Resilience Beyond Pain

Resonance Of Hope

Cheating hearts to true love

The Dream Builders Of Daveyton

Before the Bible

Ink and Imagination

Becoming A Millionaire In South Africa

Leaders of the World

Mining In Africa

Origins of Language and Civilization

Vita Nova Centre

Sisters of A cursed bloodline

Witchcraft in Africa

Ghosts of the golden city

Connected Hearts

Lost in Tokyo found in you

Table of Contents

Sibusiso Anthon Mkhwanazi

Chapter 1: Lives Interrupted

Scene 1: Sibusiso's Apartment, Johannesburg

The room is dimly lit, the shades drawn. Sibusiso sits at his cluttered desk, scrolling through emails on his laptop, sighing as he deletes one rejection after another. Bills are stacked by his computer, a reminder of his dwindling bank account.

Sibusiso: (muttering) "Another rejection... How many ways can they say 'no'? I've got the talent, I know I do. Just need one chance." (leans back in his chair, staring at the ceiling)

His phone rings, jolting him out of his thoughts. It's his friend, Kabelo.

Sibusiso: (picking up the phone) "Kabelo. Hey, man."

Kabelo: "Hey, Sbu. How you holding up, bro? I heard about the publishers pulling out..."

Sibusiso: (sighs) "Yeah. All of them. Said with the economy the way it is, they can't risk new projects. I had this one book lined up, Kabelo. It was gonna be my breakout."

Kabelo: "I know, man. I'm really sorry. But listen, maybe... I don't know, maybe it's time to consider something else?"

Sibusiso: (pauses) "Something else? You mean, like, a regular job?"

Kabelo: "Maybe. Just until things pick up again. You know, pay the bills, keep a roof over your head. This pandemic... it's crushing everyone, bro."

Sibusiso: (rubbing his face) "I hear you. But I can't shake this feeling, Kabelo. I'm meant to be a writer. But right now... right now I don't even have money for rent."

Kabelo: "Look, if you need a hand—"

Sibusiso: "Thanks, but no. I'll figure something out. I have to."

Kabelo sighs on the other end, knowing Sibusiso's stubborn streak too well.

Kabelo: "Just... don't do anything stupid, alright?"

Sibusiso: (with a forced chuckle) "Yeah. I'll keep that in mind."

They hang up, and Sibusiso stares at the screen, deep in thought. He drums his fingers, then pulls up a blank document labeled "Writer's Course."

Sibusiso: (to himself) "If people want to learn writing, why not? Just a quick online course. Nothing major... maybe I can sell a few and get back on track."

With determination, he starts typing. But somewhere, guilt flickers.

Scene 2: Nobuhle's Apartment, Johannesburg

Nobuhle stands by her window, looking out over the city she loves. Her guitar leans against the wall nearby, but she hasn't touched it in days. She grabs her phone and scrolls through her dwindling bank balance.

Nobuhle: (to herself) "I was so close. Just needed a few more gigs... just a few more."

She sighs, then gets a message from her friend Thandi.

Thandi: (in the text) *"How you holding up, Buhle? Saw your post about the cancelled album fundraiser. I'm so sorry, sis."*

Nobuhle frowns, quickly typing a response.

Nobuhle: (typing) "Yeah, thanks, Thandi. It's been rough. Don't know how I'm gonna make ends meet."

Thandi responds almost instantly.

Thandi: "You ever think of crowdfunding again? Maybe your fans would want to support you?"

Nobuhle: (murmurs) "Crowdfunding, huh?" (typing) "Not sure, Thandi. Feels wrong asking people when times are hard."

Thandi: "People love your music, Buhle. I think they'd want to help. Just be honest. Or, you know... make it sound good."

Nobuhle stares at the screen, then glances at her guitar.

Nobuhle: (to herself) "It's not scamming, right? Just... getting a little help."

She sighs, setting up a small, fake crowdfunding page titled "Support Nobuhle's Album," uploading an old cover photo and her best performance video.

Scene 3: Later That Week – Sibusiso and Nobuhle's Favorite Café, Johannesburg

Sibusiso is nursing a cup of coffee, looking downcast. Nobuhle walks in, spotting him instantly.

Nobuhle: "Sibusiso!"

Sibusiso: (manages a smile) "Buhle! Long time, hey."

They share a quick hug and settle into a booth.

Nobuhle: "You look like you haven't slept in days."

Sibusiso: (chuckles bitterly) "You're not wrong. Things have been... rough."

Nobuhle: "Same here. Lost all my gigs. Even tried crowdfunding, but people caught on. Accused me of scamming."

Sibusiso: (raises an eyebrow) "You too? I... I did something similar. Tried selling an online writing course."

Nobuhle: (eyes wide) "Did it work?"

Sibusiso: "Not exactly. People figured it out pretty fast. Now I've got no money and no reputation. You?"

Nobuhle: "My fans think I tried to con them. They're furious. I just... I just wanted a little help."

Sibusiso reaches across the table, squeezing her hand.

Sibusiso: "We both wanted to make it, Buhle. Nothing wrong with that."

They sit in silence for a moment, feeling the weight of their failed attempts.

Nobuhle: "So, what now?"

Sibusiso: (hesitates) "I was... actually thinking of leaving South Africa."

Nobuhle: (surprised) "Leaving? Where would you go?"

Sibusiso: "Tokyo. It's been a dream of mine for years. A city of reinvention, anonymity. I feel like I could start fresh there. No past. Just... me."

Nobuhle: "Tokyo..." (thoughtful) "I've always wanted to go, too. But it feels... too far. Too much."

Sibusiso: "Maybe. But I can't stay here, Buhle. There's nothing left for me here."

Nobuhle: (nodding slowly) "Maybe you're right. Sometimes a clean break is what we need."

They fall into another silence, both contemplating the possibility.

Sibusiso: "Listen, I'm leaving next week. If you ever decide to come, find me there. We could make something of ourselves... maybe."

Nobuhle: (smiling) "Maybe."

Scene 4: Sibusiso's Departure

It's the day of Sibusiso's departure. Nobuhle stands outside his apartment, watching him load his last suitcase into the car.

Nobuhle: (calling out) "You're really doing this, huh?"

Sibusiso: (smiling) "Guess so. Feels surreal."

Nobuhle: "You got a place to stay?"

Sibusiso: "Barely. Just a hostel for now. But I'll figure it out."

Nobuhle: (bittersweet) "Tokyo... must be nice. All those lights, the busy streets. Nothing like Jo'burg."

Sibusiso: "I'll miss it here. But I need this, Buhle."

Nobuhle: "I get it. Just... don't forget about me."

Sibusiso: (smiling softly) "Couldn't if I tried. Take care of yourself, okay?"

They hug tightly, holding on longer than usual. Finally, Sibusiso pulls away, his eyes showing a mix of hope and sadness.

Sibusiso: "Maybe one day, you'll join me out there."

Nobuhle: "Maybe."

Sibusiso gets into the car and gives one last wave as it pulls away. Nobuhle watches until he disappears around the corner, her heart heavy with mixed emotions.

Scene 5: Nobuhle's Decision

A few days later, Nobuhle stands by her window, looking out over the city. She opens her phone, scrolling through photos of Tokyo—the bright lights, bustling streets, serene temples. She whispers to herself.

Nobuhle: "Tokyo... a fresh start."

She glances around her apartment, small reminders of her life in Johannesburg filling the space. Her guitar rests in the corner, and for the first time in weeks, she picks it up, strumming a gentle tune. Her thoughts drift back to her conversation with Sibusiso.

Nobuhle: (thinking out loud) "Maybe he was right. Maybe I can make something of myself there."

She takes a deep breath, closing her eyes as she imagines herself performing in a Tokyo jazz club, the audience captivated by her music. Her lips curve into a smile, a spark of excitement igniting in her heart.

Nobuhle: "Alright, Tokyo... here I come."

The chapter ends with Nobuhle booking a one-way ticket to Tokyo, ready to leave behind her old life in pursuit of something unknown but filled with possibility.

This opening chapter sets up both Sibusiso's and Nobuhle's desperation, their attempts to escape hardship through questionable decisions, and finally, their longing for a fresh start in a city that promises reinvention. Each character's dialogue reveals their inner conflict, resilience, and the seeds of hope that will carry them forward as they chase their dreams in Tokyo.

Chapter 2: Arrival in Tokyo

Scene 1: Narita Airport, Tokyo

As the plane touches down, Sibusiso feels a strange mix of excitement and anxiety. He clutches his backpack tightly, his entire life condensed into a few belongings and a head full of hopes.

Sibusiso: (whispering to himself) "Alright, Sibu... here we go. New country, new start."

He steps off the plane and follows the signs through customs. The airport is buzzing with people, signs in Japanese characters, and announcements he can't understand. It's a stark reminder that he's far from home.

At the customs counter, the officer gestures for his passport. Sibusiso hands it over, trying to keep calm.

Customs Officer: (in broken English) "Purpose of visit?"

Sibusiso: "I... I'm here to work. I'm a writer."

The officer raises an eyebrow, stamping his passport with a neutral expression.

Customs Officer: "Welcome to Japan."

Sibusiso nods, taking back his passport and feeling a surge of relief as he walks through the gate, officially in Tokyo.

Scene 2: Arrival at the Hostel

Sibusiso exits the train station into the heart of Tokyo. Neon lights flash from every angle, signs in Japanese illuminate the bustling streets, and people move with an intensity he's never seen before. He checks the address on his phone, clutching his worn-out suitcase as he navigates the streets.

Sibusiso: (to himself) "This city... it's massive. Feels like... I'm on another planet."

After wandering a few blocks, he finally finds his hostel, a small, cramped building squeezed between a ramen shop and a convenience store. He enters, finding the reception desk just inside the door.

Receptionist: (with a friendly smile) "Konnichiwa! Welcome."

Sibusiso: "Uh... Konnichiwa! I have a booking here? Name's Sibusiso."

The receptionist nods, checking her computer, then hands him a small key with the number "305" on it.

Receptionist: "Room three-oh-five. Elevator that way."

He nods his thanks and heads up to his room. Opening the door, he finds a tiny space, barely big enough for a bed and a desk. The walls are plain, and there's a small window overlooking a narrow alley.

Sibusiso: (sighing) "Well... it's not much, but it's mine. For now."

He places his suitcase on the bed, looking around the room, the reality of his situation settling in.

Sibusiso: (to himself) "Tokyo's not Jo'burg, that's for sure. Everything's different here. Just gotta get used to it."

Scene 3: Exploring the City

The next morning, Sibusiso steps out into the bustling streets of Shibuya. He marvels at the crowds, the high-rises, the flashing advertisements, and the crisp, organized chaos of Tokyo. He stumbles upon Shibuya Crossing, where hundreds of people cross in every direction.

Sibusiso: (awed) "This place... it's like nothing I've ever seen. I can't believe people actually live like this every day."

He tries to order a coffee at a small café but quickly realizes the language barrier is more challenging than he anticipated. After fumbling through a few words in English and gestures, the barista smiles politely and hands him a small cup.

Sibusiso: "Arigatou... I think that's thank you."

The barista nods, giving a small bow. Sibusiso takes his coffee and sits by the window, watching people stream by.

Sibusiso: (to himself) "Back home, a place like this would be swarming with noise, people talking. But here, it's so... quiet. Even with all these people, no one's shouting, no one's rushing."

He pulls out his notebook, trying to capture his feelings in words, but the inspiration doesn't come. He closes the notebook in frustration.

Sibusiso: "Come on, Sibu. You're in Tokyo. If you can't write here, where can you?"

Scene 4: The Language Barrier

Later, Sibusiso tries to go grocery shopping at a nearby convenience store. He stares at the shelves, overwhelmed by the unfamiliar packaging and Japanese characters.

Sibusiso: (muttering) "Okay... is this rice or... flour? I can't read any of this."

He awkwardly picks up a few items, hoping they're what he needs. At the register, the cashier says something in rapid Japanese.

Cashier: "Ichi man yon hyaku desu."

Sibusiso: (confused) "Uh... sorry, I... don't understand."

The cashier repeats it slower, but Sibusiso still has no idea. He hands over a large bill, hoping it's enough. The cashier takes it, gives him change, and smiles politely.

Sibusiso: "Arigatou." (to himself) "This language... it's like music, but I don't understand the tune."

Scene 5: An Encounter with Hiroshi

That evening, Sibusiso returns to the hostel's common room, hoping to meet other travelers. He sees a young man with glasses, sitting with his laptop, who gives him a friendly nod.

Hiroshi: "Hey there. You new here?"

Sibusiso: (relieved to hear English) "Yeah, just arrived yesterday. I'm Sibusiso."

Hiroshi: "I'm Hiroshi. Nice to meet you. Where you from?"

Sibusiso: "South Africa. I'm a writer... or at least, I'm trying to be."

Hiroshi: "That's amazing! Writing in Tokyo must be... different."

Sibusiso: (chuckling) "That's one way to put it. Honestly, I'm struggling. Everything feels... foreign."

Hiroshi: "You're not alone. Tokyo can be overwhelming, especially if you're here to start something new. But hey, at least you're brave enough to try."

Sibusiso: "Thanks. I just... I just want to make it. I have big dreams, but right now, they feel far away."

They talk for a while, and Hiroshi gives him a few tips on adjusting to life in Tokyo and suggests places where Sibusiso might find some inspiration.

Scene 6: Facing the Cost of Living

A few days later, Sibusiso sits in his room, looking over his finances. Tokyo is more expensive than he imagined, and his initial budget is rapidly shrinking.

Sibusiso: (to himself, counting his remaining cash) "Alright... I've got enough for rent and maybe two weeks of food. This is... going fast."

He pulls out his laptop, searching for freelance writing gigs or anything that might help him make some money. However, most opportunities require fluent Japanese or more connections than he has.

Sibusiso: (frustrated) "Come on, there has to be something. Tokyo's supposed to be the city of opportunity, right?"

His phone buzzes with a message from Hiroshi, inviting him to a local writers' meetup.

Sibusiso: (murmuring) "A writers' meetup... maybe I'll meet someone who can help."

Scene 7: The Writers' Meetup

The next evening, Sibusiso arrives at a small café filled with writers, mostly Japanese, some foreigners. He takes a seat at a table, looking around nervously.

Hiroshi: (coming over) "Sibusiso! You made it."

Sibusiso: "Thanks for inviting me, Hiroshi. It's... it's nice to be around writers."

They join a conversation where people are sharing their experiences of living in Tokyo. Sibusiso listens, realizing he's not the only one struggling.

Writer 1: "When I first moved here, I was overwhelmed. Tokyo is beautiful but relentless."

Writer 2: "Right? It's like the city takes from you before it gives back."

Sibusiso: (nodding) "That's exactly how I feel. Like I'm being tested or something."

They all laugh knowingly, and Sibusiso feels a sense of comfort, like he's part of a community.

Hiroshi: "Just keep going, Sibusiso. Tokyo has a way of opening doors... eventually."

Scene 8: Finding Inspiration

A few nights later, Sibusiso takes a late-night walk through the city, trying to process everything he's experienced so far. He wanders through a quiet temple garden, breathing in the calm atmosphere.

Sibusiso: (thinking) "Maybe Tokyo's not about making it big right away. Maybe it's about learning... adapting."

He takes out his notebook, finally feeling the urge to write. Sitting on a bench, he jots down his thoughts.

Sibusiso: (writing) "Tokyo isn't just a city. It's a test. It strips you down to nothing, forces you to confront every part of yourself. But maybe, in that emptiness, you find who you really are."

As he writes, he feels a small spark of hope reignite within him. For the first time since arriving, he feels like he belongs, like Tokyo is becoming a part of him.

Chapter 3: Nobuhle's Journey

Scene 1: Arrival at Narita Airport

Months after Sibusiso, Nobuhle finally arrives in Tokyo. She steps off the plane, clutching her carry-on bag and a folder filled with music sheets and notes. As she enters the crowded airport terminal, the magnitude of her decision hits her.

Nobuhle: (whispering to herself) "You did it, Nobuhle. You're here... in Tokyo."

She takes a deep breath, scanning the sea of unfamiliar faces around her. Despite the thrill of being in a new city, a flicker of uncertainty crosses her face.

Nobuhle: "Alright... first things first. Find the place I'm staying."

She quickly makes her way through customs, her confidence fading slightly as she realizes just how foreign everything feels. Her phone buzzes with a message from her friend back home.

Friend: *"You're really doing it, hey! Tokyo, girl! Can't wait to hear your music all the way over there."*

Nobuhle: (texting back) *"I'll make it happen, just wait."*

With that, she heads out into the bustling Tokyo evening, determined to make her mark.

Scene 2: First Night in Tokyo

Later that night, Nobuhle checks into a small, modest hostel. She sits on the edge of the bed, exhausted but too wired to sleep. The distant sounds of the city pulse through the window.

Nobuhle: (to herself) "Tokyo... you're even louder than I imagined."

She picks up her guitar, strumming softly, her fingers finding familiar chords. The music fills the quiet of the room, grounding her for a moment. But her mind is restless, her thoughts swirling between her dreams and the reality she's now facing.

Nobuhle: "Okay. First step: find a place to perform. I need a stage. And maybe... someone who believes in me."

Scene 3: The Jazz Club

A few days later, Nobuhle is wandering through the streets of Shinjuku when she stumbles upon a small jazz club nestled in an alley. A sign hangs above the door, reading "Blue Moon Jazz." She pauses, the hum of saxophone music drifting out into the street, drawing her closer.

Inside, the club is dimly lit, with tables scattered around a small stage. A few patrons are seated, sipping drinks, and watching a trio of musicians performing with an effortless cool. Behind the bar, an older woman with striking silver hair watches the stage with a serene, yet intense gaze.

Intrigued, Nobuhle approaches the bar.

Nobuhle: "Excuse me... is this your place?"

The woman looks her up and down, her eyes sharp and discerning.

Mika Saito: "It is. You're not from around here, are you?"

Nobuhle: "No... I'm from South Africa. Just arrived. I'm a musician. I was hoping... maybe there's a place for me here?"

Mika raises an eyebrow, considering her.

Mika Saito: "South Africa... interesting. You play jazz?"

Nobuhle: (nodding) "And some soul... R&B... whatever speaks to the heart."

Mika looks her over for a long moment, her gaze lingering on Nobuhle's worn guitar case.

Mika Saito: "Show me what you've got. There's an open mic tomorrow night. If you're any good, we'll see where it goes."

Nobuhle: "Thank you! I won't disappoint you."

As Nobuhle turns to leave, Mika stops her.

Mika Saito: "Tokyo isn't an easy city, especially for someone like you. It'll test you, break you down. But if you're strong enough... it might just build you back up."

Nobuhle: (smiling) "I've faced hard times before. This is just a new stage."

Scene 4: Open Mic Night

The next evening, Nobuhle arrives at Blue Moon Jazz, her heart pounding with a mix of excitement and nerves. The club is packed, and the murmurs of conversation fill the air as people settle in for the open mic performances.

When it's finally her turn, she takes a deep breath, steps onto the stage, and adjusts the microphone. She strums her guitar, the opening chords filling the space, and then she begins to sing.

Her voice, rich and soulful, draws the audience into her world. She sings about loss, about hope, about the resilience it takes to keep going. When she finishes, there's a moment of silence, followed by enthusiastic applause.

From behind the bar, Mika watches, a faint smile on her lips.

Mika Saito: (to herself) "She has it... that spark."

After the performance, Nobuhle approaches the bar, her face glowing with excitement.

Nobuhle: "So... how did I do?"

Mika Saito: "Not bad, South Africa. You have a good voice... and something real behind it."

Nobuhle: (beaming) "Thank you! I've always felt music is... it's my way of telling stories."

Mika Saito: "You're welcome to play here. And I can introduce you to a few people in the industry. But remember, Tokyo's a tough crowd. They'll love you one minute, and turn their back the next."

Nobuhle nods, determined.

Nobuhle: "I'll give it my best, no matter what."

Mika looks at her, as if measuring her resilience.

Mika Saito: "Good. You'll need that fire."

Scene 5: Mentorship Begins

Over the next few weeks, Nobuhle plays at Blue Moon Jazz regularly, slowly building a small following. Mika watches over her performances, occasionally offering feedback. One night, after the club has closed, Mika sits with Nobuhle, sharing a glass of wine.

Mika Saito: "Tell me, Nobuhle... what brought you all the way here?"

Nobuhle: (sighing) "Back in South Africa, things were... tough. I lost my job, tried a few... let's say 'questionable' things to get by, but nothing worked out. I came here because... I needed a fresh start. A real one."

Mika nods, listening intently.

Mika Saito: "I understand. Tokyo has a way of attracting people who need to reinvent themselves."

Nobuhle: "Did it help you, coming here?"

Mika's face softens, a hint of sadness in her eyes.

Mika Saito: "In a way. But Tokyo also took a lot from me. I came here young, filled with dreams. The city embraced me... but it also made me sacrifice parts of myself I wasn't prepared to lose."

Nobuhle: "But you stayed."

Mika Saito: "I did. Because even with the pain, there's a magic in this city. It gives you a chance to become someone new."

Nobuhle sips her wine, contemplating Mika's words.

Nobuhle: "I guess that's what I'm hoping for. A chance to be... more than I was."

S cene 6: Gaining Confidence
As weeks turn into months, Nobuhle grows more comfortable in Tokyo and gains confidence in her performances. She attracts a small but loyal audience at Blue Moon Jazz, and Mika introduces her to other musicians and artists in the city. One night, after a particularly powerful performance, Mika pulls her aside.

Mika Saito: "You've come a long way since that first night, Nobuhle. You're starting to find your voice."

Nobuhle: (smiling) "Thanks to you, Mika. I couldn't have done it without your guidance."

Mika Saito: "Remember, Tokyo's not the end of your journey. It's just the beginning."

Scene 7: Facing a Challenge

One evening, a talent scout from a well-known record label attends one of Nobuhle's performances. After the show, he approaches her, handing her his card.

Talent Scout: "I'm impressed, Nobuhle. We're looking for fresh talent, and I think you have what it takes. Let's talk about a potential deal."

Excited, Nobuhle takes the card, barely able to contain her excitement. But when she shares the news with Mika, her mentor's reaction is unexpected.

Mika Saito: "Be careful with those types. They promise the world, but it comes at a price."

Nobuhle: "But Mika, this could be my big break!"

Mika Saito: (sighing) "Just remember, Nobuhle... sometimes success in Tokyo is as fleeting as a cherry blossom. Think carefully before you sign anything."

Nobuhle nods, her excitement tempered by Mika's warning.

Scene 8: Reflection

That night, Nobuhle returns to her room, thinking over Mika's words. She pulls out her guitar, playing a soft, melancholic tune.

Nobuhle: (to herself) "Tokyo gave me this chance... but at what cost? I came here to find myself, not to lose it."

She looks out the window, watching the lights of the city flicker against the night sky. Tokyo's allure is strong, but she's beginning to understand that every choice she makes here will shape her future.

Chapter 4: A Chance Encounter

Scene 1: Sibusiso Arrives at Blue Moon Jazz

Sibusiso walks down a narrow street in Shinjuku, feeling the hum of Tokyo nightlife around him. He's heard about Blue Moon Jazz from a friend who recommended the club for its soulful, raw performances. Curious and craving a taste of home, he steps inside.

The club is dimly lit, with the low hum of conversation blending with the soft notes of jazz from the stage. He settles at the bar, ordering a drink, and looks around. Just then, a familiar melody fills the room, drawing his attention to the stage.

It's Nobuhle, singing with her heart and soul.

Sibusiso: (muttering to himself) "No way... Nobuhle?"

He watches her, mesmerized. As she sings, Nobuhle's eyes wander over the crowd, and then she sees him. Her voice falters for a split second as she recognizes Sibusiso, sitting right in front of her.

Nobuhle: (thinking) "Sibusiso... here? In Tokyo?"

She quickly regains her composure and finishes her song. The audience erupts in applause as she steps off stage, making her way toward the bar where Sibusiso is waiting.

Scene 2: Reunited at Last

Nobuhle approaches him cautiously, almost as if she's worried he might disappear.

Nobuhle: "Sibusiso... is it really you?"

Sibusiso: (smiling) "Nobuhle Zungu, live and in Tokyo. What are the odds?"

They embrace, laughing in disbelief. Nobuhle takes a seat beside him, and they order drinks.

Nobuhle: "I thought I'd left everyone behind. How did you end up here?"

Sibusiso: (chuckling) "It's a long story. South Africa... well, it wasn't kind to me. I needed a fresh start."

Nobuhle: "I get it. Things weren't great for me, either. COVID took a lot away, you know?"

They both pause, a shared understanding between them. There's a lot they aren't saying, memories of desperate times left unspoken.

Sibusiso: "So... you're a musician here?"

Nobuhle: "Yeah. I sing at this club, trying to make something of myself. And you?"

Sibusiso: "Writing, like always. Trying to piece things together."

Scene 3: Reminiscing on the Past

They spend the next hour catching up on each other's lives, laughing about old memories from back in South Africa. As they chat, there's a weight in the air, an understanding that both have been through struggles that have shaped them.

Nobuhle: "Remember when we used to talk about leaving South Africa, chasing big dreams somewhere out there? It felt like... just a fantasy."

Sibusiso: "And now here we are, halfway around the world, doing exactly that. Funny how life works."

Nobuhle: (smiling) "Tokyo feels like a strange kind of second chance, doesn't it?"

Sibusiso: "It does. And seeing you here... it's like a reminder that we're stronger than we think."

Scene 4: Hidden Secrets

They sit in a comfortable silence for a moment, sipping their drinks. But behind their smiles and laughter, each is carrying secrets. Sibusiso thinks back to his failed scams back in South Africa, the desperation that had driven him to leave. Nobuhle has her own memories of risky choices she'd rather forget.

Nobuhle: (after a pause) "Tokyo's been good, but it hasn't been easy. Sometimes I think... it's like running from one storm to another."

Sibusiso: "Yeah, I get that. But maybe this is our chance to make something of ourselves. To do things right."

Nobuhle nods, a glint of sadness in her eyes, as if she's thinking of everything she's left behind.

Nobuhle: "It's strange, though. Even after all this time, I feel like there are things I can't let go of."

Sibusiso: "Maybe that's why we're both here, on the other side of the world. A chance to start fresh."

Scene 5: The Beginning of a Friendship

As the night goes on, their laughter fills the small club, and they begin to relax. Nobuhle shares stories of her life in Tokyo, of her late nights at Blue Moon Jazz, and her dreams of becoming something more than just a struggling musician.

Sibusiso: "I've got to say, Nobuhle... seeing you on that stage, you're incredible. You're not just surviving here; you're thriving."

Nobuhle: (blushing) "Thanks, Sibu. It's hard sometimes. But music... it's the only thing that's ever made sense to me."

Sibusiso: "And you're doing it. You're living the dream, even if it doesn't always feel like it."

Nobuhle: "And you? What about your writing?"

Sibusiso: "Same thing. It's been a struggle, but Tokyo's given me a new perspective. Maybe... maybe I can write a story worth reading."

Scene 6: Parting Ways, but with Hope

As the night draws to a close, they step outside, the cool Tokyo air wrapping around them. They look up at the city lights, both feeling a little less alone than they did before.

Nobuhle: "Thank you, Sibu. I didn't realize how much I needed to see a familiar face."

Sibusiso: "Same here. Tokyo's a big place... but maybe we can make it feel a little smaller. If you need anything, you know where to find me."

Nobuhle: (smiling) "I might just take you up on that. Don't disappear on me now."

Sibusiso: (grinning) "I'm not going anywhere."

They part ways, each walking off into the Tokyo night with a renewed sense of purpose and comfort. For the first time in a long time, they feel a connection, a reminder that they're not alone in this vast, foreign city.

As Nobuhle disappears around the corner, Sibusiso watches her go, a quiet smile on his face.

Sibusiso: (to himself) "Maybe Tokyo isn't just about running away... maybe it's about finding something worth staying for."

Chapter 5: Finding Allies

Scene 1: Sibusiso Meets Yuto Tanaka

Sibusiso sits at a coffee shop in Tokyo, looking over his notebook. He's been struggling to find an outlet for his writing, frustrated but determined. Just then, a Japanese man in his early thirties sits beside him, noticing the stack of papers covered in scribbled ideas.

Yuto: (smiling) "You must be a writer. Only writers look this frustrated while staring at blank pages."

Sibusiso glances up, surprised by the casual remark, and chuckles.

Sibusiso: "Is it that obvious? It's been a while since I had to start from scratch."

Yuto: "Tokyo has a way of doing that to people. Yuto Tanaka, literary agent."

He extends a hand, and Sibusiso shakes it eagerly.

Sibusiso: "Sibusiso Mkhwanazi. I'm... well, trying to write something that matters. Not sure what yet."

Yuto: (nodding) "Good stories find their own way to the page. It sounds like you've got something special in mind; maybe I can help you find a direction."

They chat over coffee, and Sibusiso shares bits of his life, his dreams, and the struggles that led him to Tokyo. Yuto listens intently, nodding at the right moments.

Yuto: "You know, Tokyo's tough for foreigners, but if you can adapt, it has a way of opening doors. Have you thought of writing something about your experiences here? About what it's like to be caught between worlds?"

Sibusiso: (thoughtful) "It crossed my mind. But I wasn't sure anyone would care."

Yuto: "Stories of transformation resonate everywhere. If you're interested, I'd like to work with you. I think we could create something powerful together."

Sibusiso's eyes light up with hope. This could be the opportunity he's been waiting for.

Sibusiso: "Thank you, Yuto. I think this might just be what I needed."

Scene 2: Nobuhle Encounters Hana Yoshida

Back at Blue Moon Jazz, Nobuhle is preparing for her evening performance when she notices a young Japanese woman sitting in the front row. The woman watches her closely, almost like a challenge. After the set, the woman approaches.

Hana: "You're good. Nobuhle Zungu, right?"

Nobuhle: (surprised) "Yes, that's me. And you are?"

Hana: "Hana Yoshida. Singer, like you. I've been around this scene long enough to know it's rare to see fresh talent in places like this."

Nobuhle feels both flattered and wary, sensing something competitive in Hana's gaze.

Nobuhle: "Thanks. I'm still getting used to Tokyo, to be honest. It's a lot to take in."

Hana: (laughing) "I get that. The industry here... it's ruthless. You'll meet people who'll promise you the world, but most of them are just looking for someone new to profit off of. Be careful who you trust."

Nobuhle nods, feeling the weight of Hana's warning. She's seen hints of that in her own brief time here, but it's refreshing to hear it openly acknowledged.

Nobuhle: "Thanks for the advice. I'm learning to keep my guard up."

Hana: "Good. I'm not saying don't trust anyone. Just... pick your allies carefully."

They exchange numbers, and Nobuhle watches Hana walk away, feeling both inspired and a little wary. She knows Hana sees her as potential competition, but perhaps that rivalry can push her to be better.

Scene 3: Growing Trust Between Sibusiso and Yuto
A week later, Sibusiso meets Yuto at his small office. Yuto's walls are lined with books from different genres and languages, and there's a warmth to the space that instantly puts Sibusiso at ease.

Yuto: (handing Sibusiso a manuscript) "I reviewed your first few pages. You've got something unique here. But you're holding back."

Sibusiso: "Holding back?"

Yuto: "Tokyo has a way of challenging people, and I sense a lot of untold stories in you. Don't be afraid to dig deeper, to show the struggle. Readers want honesty."

Sibusiso nods, inspired by Yuto's words. This is the kind of encouragement he's been missing.

Sibusiso: "Thank you, Yuto. I think... I needed to hear that."

Yuto smiles, his expression a mixture of encouragement and excitement.

Yuto: "Tokyo has room for voices like yours, Sibusiso. Let's make sure the world hears it."

Their connection deepens as Sibusiso starts trusting Yuto more, seeing him as a genuine mentor and ally. With Yuto's help, he feels closer to finding his voice in this city.

Scene 4: Nobuhle's Growing Ambition

Nobuhle meets with Hana a few times after performances. Hana shares stories of her own struggles, from deceptive managers to harsh critics, often spinning them as lessons Nobuhle should learn from. But Nobuhle senses a subtle edge in Hana's tone, a reminder that they are in the same competitive field.

Hana: "You've got something special, Nobuhle. But talent isn't enough. Here, you need to stand out or get swallowed up."

Nobuhle: "So how do you do it? Stand out, I mean."

Hana: (smirking) "Stay sharp. Make friends, sure, but don't rely on anyone. Tokyo rewards those who can adapt, who don't let their guard down."

Nobuhle listens carefully, noting the intensity in Hana's words. She's grateful for the guidance but begins to understand Hana's competitive spirit is rooted in survival.

Nobuhle: "I appreciate the advice, Hana. I won't forget it."

Hana smiles, but there's a flicker of tension between them now, an unspoken understanding that they both want to rise, and that there's room for only a few at the top.

Scene 5: Sibusiso and Nobuhle Reflecting on New Friendships

Later that night, Sibusiso and Nobuhle meet up for a late dinner, both eager to share the new connections they've made.

Nobuhle: "I met this singer, Hana. She's talented, but there's something... competitive about her. She warned me about trusting people in this industry."

Sibusiso: "I get that. I met a literary agent, Yuto. He's been pushing me to dig deeper in my writing, to be honest about my experiences. But I'm starting to wonder... is he looking out for me, or for his own career?"

Nobuhle: "It's hard, Sibu. I don't know if I can trust Hana either, but I'm learning from her, at least."

They sit in a thoughtful silence, realizing that while Tokyo has given them allies, it's also given them reasons to stay cautious.

Sibusiso: "Maybe that's what Tokyo is teaching us. To learn from people without losing ourselves."

Nobuhle: "Exactly. To be wise enough to take what we need, but still remember why we came here."

They raise their glasses in a quiet toast, both determined to navigate Tokyo's challenges on their own terms, yet grateful for each other's support.

Chapter 6: A Growing Attraction

Scene 1: **A Late-Night Stroll**

It's late evening, and Sibusiso and Nobuhle are walking together through one of Tokyo's quiet neighborhoods. They've just finished dinner at a tiny ramen shop and are now strolling along, watching the city lights reflect off the nearby canal. The air is cool, and they're comfortable in each other's presence.

Nobuhle: "It's hard to believe we're here, you know? Two kids from South Africa, walking around in Tokyo."

Sibusiso: (smiling) "I know. I still wake up some days, thinking I'm back home. Then I hear the Tokyo traffic, and I'm reminded where I am."

They laugh softly, both aware of how far they've come—and of the heavy past they carry with them.

Nobuhle: "Do you... ever feel like you're running from something? I mean, why Tokyo?"

Sibusiso: (pausing) "Maybe I am running. Or maybe I'm searching for something. A fresh start, I guess. And you?"

Nobuhle: (looking away) "I'm not sure. I came here hoping to leave parts of my past behind, but... I think I brought it all with me."

They fall into silence, their unspoken secrets thickening the air between them.

Scene 2: Growing Closer

Over the next few weeks, they spend more and more time together, meeting at cafes, visiting art galleries, and sharing quiet moments in hidden parts of the city. They find comfort in each other, understanding the struggles of being far from home.

One afternoon, they're sitting on a bench in Ueno Park, watching cherry blossoms fall around them.

Sibusiso: "I feel like I can talk to you about anything, Nobuhle. It's... different."

Nobuhle: "Same here. I don't usually open up to people, but with you... it's like I don't have to explain myself."

Sibusiso: (grinning) "Maybe it's because we both have skeletons in the closet. It's easier to connect with someone who gets it."

She laughs, but there's a hint of sadness in her eyes.

Nobuhle: "You're right. But maybe it's also because we want to be better versions of ourselves here, right?"

Sibusiso: "Yeah. A fresh start."

They share a lingering look, both feeling the pull but too cautious to give in completely.

Scene 3: An Unexpected Moment

One evening after Nobuhle's performance at Blue Moon Jazz, Sibusiso waits for her at the bar. The crowd has thinned out, and she's finishing up with the band. When she's done, she joins him at the bar, and they sit together, both a little tipsy from the celebratory drinks.

Nobuhle: (leaning on the bar) "You know, I never thought I'd see you here, cheering me on. It's... nice."

Sibusiso: (smiling) "It feels right, doesn't it? Being here, supporting each other."

She nods, her eyes meeting his, and for a moment, it feels like the rest of the world fades away. The space between them seems to shrink, and they lean in, almost as if drawn together by some unseen force.

Sibusiso: (whispering) "Nobuhle..."

Just as he's about to close the gap, she pulls back, a flicker of hesitation in her eyes.

Nobuhle: "I... I can't. Not yet."

Sibusiso nods, trying to hide his disappointment.

Sibusiso: "I understand. We've both been through a lot. No rush."

They share a bittersweet smile, and though they don't say it out loud, they both know their connection is undeniable, yet complicated by their pasts.

Scene 4: Haunted by Regrets

Later that night, Sibusiso returns to his apartment. He sits alone, replaying the evening in his mind, wishing he hadn't held back but also afraid of the consequences if he had let himself fall completely.

He thinks back to the failed schemes in South Africa, the small, desperate crimes he'd tried in moments of hopelessness. The shame of those memories still clings to him, making him feel unworthy of someone like Nobuhle.

Sibusiso: (murmuring to himself) "What if she knew? What if she knew everything I've done?"

Meanwhile, across town, Nobuhle sits by her window, looking out at the city lights, haunted by similar thoughts. Her own past mistakes and moments of weakness weigh heavily on her heart, and she fears that Sibusiso, if he ever knew the full story, would look at her differently.

Nobuhle: (whispering) "I can't drag him into my past. He deserves better."

Both are caught in a cycle of guilt and self-doubt, afraid to reveal too much of themselves, yet longing for the comfort only the other can provide.

Scene 5: Testing the Waters

In the days that follow, Sibusiso and Nobuhle continue to spend time together, but an invisible barrier keeps them from getting too close. They joke and laugh, but the tension between them is undeniable.

One evening, as they're walking back from dinner, Sibusiso decides to try breaking down some of the walls.

Sibusiso: "Nobuhle, I know we both have things we don't talk about. But if you ever want to... I'm here. I won't judge."

Nobuhle: (pausing, touched) "Thank you, Sibu. That means more than you know."

She considers telling him about the tough times she went through, the times she felt cornered into making difficult choices. But something holds her back. Instead, she squeezes his hand, grateful for his understanding, even if they both remain guarded.

Nobuhle: "Maybe one day, we can leave it all behind. Just... focus on what's ahead."

Sibusiso: "Yeah. One day."

They continue walking in silence, comforted by each other's presence, yet aware that both are hiding shadows they're not ready to reveal.

Scene 6: A Tender Goodbye

Later, Sibusiso walks Nobuhle to her apartment. They stand at her door, lingering, neither wanting the night to end.

Sibusiso: "Thanks for tonight. I feel like... I don't know. I feel lighter."

Nobuhle: (smiling) "Me too. It's like you're the only one who gets it."

There's a long, quiet pause as they look at each other. Sibusiso reaches out and gently tucks a stray piece of hair behind her ear. The touch is brief, but it sends a spark between them.

Sibusiso: "Goodnight, Nobuhle."

Nobuhle: (softly) "Goodnight, Sibusiso."

He turns to leave, but she stops him, a determined look in her eyes.

Nobuhle: "Wait... don't go just yet."

She pulls him into a gentle hug, holding him close, as if drawing strength from him. He wraps his arms around her, both of them breathing in the warmth of the moment.

Nobuhle: (whispering) "Whatever we've been through... I think we're going to be okay. Together."

Sibusiso pulls back slightly, looking into her eyes.

Sibusiso: "Yeah. Together."

They part ways with a lingering look, the promise of something deeper simmering between them, even as they hold back, uncertain of what the future might bring.

Chapter 7: Unwanted Ties

Scene 1: A Familiar Face

It's a bustling evening in Shibuya. Sibusiso is weaving through the crowd on his way to meet Nobuhle for dinner when he feels a tap on his shoulder. He turns around, stunned to see Jared "Jay" Mafela grinning back at him, hands stuffed in his leather jacket pockets.

Sibusiso: (shocked) "Jay? What... what are you doing here?"

Jay: (chuckling) "Come on, man, no hug for an old friend? Didn't think I'd let you leave without saying goodbye forever, did you?"

Sibusiso hesitates, then gives Jay a quick, uncomfortable hug. Memories of their past together—the schemes, the risky plans—flash in his mind, and he can feel his stomach tighten.

Sibusiso: "How did you find me here? Tokyo's the last place I expected to see you."

Jay: "Took a bit of digging, but hey, you left enough breadcrumbs. Figured you wouldn't mind a little visit from someone who remembers the real you."

Sibusiso feels a chill. He thought he'd left his old life—and everyone in it—far behind.

Sibusiso: "Look, Jay, whatever you're here for... I'm not interested."

Jay: (smirking) "Who said anything about business? Can't a guy just visit an old friend? Let's grab a drink."

Sibusiso considers refusing, but he nods reluctantly, feeling there's no easy way to shake off Jay without causing a scene.

Scene 2: Temptation

They settle in a small bar, with Jay talking animatedly about his travels since leaving South Africa. Sibusiso listens half-heartedly, feeling unease creeping in with every word.

Jay: "Tokyo, man. Full of opportunity if you know where to look. And you do, don't you?"

Sibusiso shakes his head, trying to keep his voice firm.

Sibusiso: "Jay, I'm here to start over. I don't want anything to do with... the old life."

Jay: "Relax, Sibu. You think I came all the way here to mess up your fresh start? Just a little business on the side, easy money. I've got connections now, people who can make things happen without us getting our hands dirty."

Sibusiso clenches his fists under the table, feeling the familiar tug of desperation mixed with dread.

Sibusiso: "I'm serious, Jay. I'm done. I came here for a reason. You should, too."

Jay laughs, waving a hand dismissively.

Jay: "Don't act like you don't miss it. The thrill, the cash—quicker than any nine-to-five job. We used to dream about stuff like this, remember? You and me, partners in crime."

Sibusiso's mind races. He remembers the debt he's racked up trying to make it in Tokyo, the bills piling up, the doors closing in his face. For a split second, Jay's offer seems tempting—but he quickly shakes it off.

Sibusiso: "That was then. I'm not that guy anymore."

Jay leans forward, his eyes gleaming.

Jay: "Alright, but think about it. I'll be around. Tokyo isn't as big as it seems."

Scene 3: Disruption

Days pass, but Jay's presence lingers in Sibusiso's mind, disrupting his peace and casting a shadow over his new life. He tries to focus on his writing and his growing relationship with Nobuhle, but there's a gnawing feeling he can't shake.

One evening, as he's walking Nobuhle home after another night at Blue Moon Jazz, he notices Jay across the street, watching them. Sibusiso stiffens, hoping Nobuhle doesn't see him.

Nobuhle: (noticing his tension) "You okay? You've been on edge these past few days."

Sibusiso: (forcing a smile) "Yeah, just... a lot on my mind, I guess. Trying to make it here isn't easy."

Nobuhle nods, understanding, but gives him a searching look.

Nobuhle: "If you ever need to talk, I'm here. We're in this together, remember?"

Sibusiso's heart sinks, knowing he's keeping secrets from her. He squeezes her hand but says nothing.

Scene 4: Confrontation

A few nights later, Jay shows up at Sibusiso's apartment unannounced, his grin as confident as ever.

Jay: "Thought I'd check in on my old pal. Make sure you're still surviving without my help."

Sibusiso: (annoyed) "Jay, I told you I'm not interested. Stop showing up like this."

Jay shrugs, unaffected by Sibusiso's tone.

Jay: "Look, man, I get it. You're trying to go straight, be the good guy. But life here is expensive, isn't it? You could use some extra cash."

Sibusiso crosses his arms, struggling to keep his voice steady.

Sibusiso: "I don't want to be dragged back into that life. I'm building something new here."

Jay: "Sure you are. But new dreams don't pay Tokyo rent, do they? Come on, Sibu. One job. Quick and clean. Then I'm out of your hair."

Sibusiso's resolve wavers for a moment, memories of their past adventures flashing in his mind. He quickly pushes them aside.

Sibusiso: "No, Jay. I'm serious. I don't want this."

Jay's face hardens, a hint of irritation breaking through his charm.

Jay: "Fine. But don't come running to me when you're struggling to make ends meet. Just remember—Tokyo is a lonely place if you don't have friends."

Jay turns and leaves, slamming the door behind him. Sibusiso slumps against the door, feeling the weight of the decision he just made.

Scene 5: The Pressure Builds

Over the next few days, Sibusiso tries to focus on his work, but Jay's words linger in his mind. The bills keep coming, and his freelance work isn't paying enough to keep up. He grows more distant from Nobuhle, afraid that his struggles and past will pull her into his world of complications.

One evening, Nobuhle confronts him as they walk home after her performance.

Nobuhle: "Sibu, what's going on? You've been so distracted lately. If there's something wrong, just tell me."

Sibusiso hesitates, his mind racing. He wants to confide in her, but he's terrified of pushing her away.

Sibusiso: "I... I'm just under a lot of pressure. Life here is harder than I thought."

Nobuhle: (softly) "You're not alone. I'm here, and I want to help, whatever it is."

Sibusiso nods, touched by her support, but he knows that his past with Jay is something she wouldn't understand—or forgive.

Sibusiso: "Thanks, Buhle. I just need some time to sort things out."

She nods, though her worry is clear. Sibusiso feels torn, knowing that the more he distances himself from Jay, the more he risks losing Nobuhle's trust.

Scene 6: Jay's Ultimatum

Late one night, Sibusiso returns to his apartment to find a note slipped under his door. It's from Jay, urging him to meet at a bar near Shinjuku.

Sibusiso considers ignoring it, but a nagging feeling pulls him there. When he arrives, he finds Jay waiting, looking far less friendly than before.

Jay: "Listen, Sibu, I didn't want it to come to this, but you're leaving me no choice. I've got a lot riding on this job, and I need someone I can trust."

Sibusiso: (angry) "And you think forcing me is going to make me trust you?"

Jay: "I'm not forcing you, man. I'm giving you a chance to help yourself out. And if you don't... well, Tokyo isn't as safe as you might think."

Sibusiso clenches his fists, realizing Jay won't take no for an answer. He's trapped between protecting his new life and the dangerous ties of his old one.

Chapter 8: Rivalries and Rumors

Scene 1: Rising Tensions at Blue Moon Jazz

It's a packed night at Blue Moon Jazz. Nobuhle is on stage, captivating the audience with her soulful performance. In the dimly lit corner, Ayame Suzuki, a well-known singer at the club, watches with a sharp, calculating gaze.

Ayame: (muttering to herself) "Look at her... soaking up all the attention. She thinks she can just walk in here and take over?"

Ayame turns to her friend, Rika, who's sitting beside her, watching Nobuhle's performance with a neutral expression.

Rika: "Ayame, you're overthinking it. Nobuhle's good, but she's not taking anything from you."

Ayame: (scowling) "Not yet, but she will if I let her. People are already talking about her like she's the next big thing. I can't let her ruin what I've built."

Ayame's expression hardens as she continues to watch Nobuhle, who's oblivious to the jealousy brewing in the room.

Scene 2: A Plan Takes Shape

Later that night, after Nobuhle's set, Ayame follows her into the dressing room. Nobuhle smiles when she notices Ayame, oblivious to the tension.

Nobuhle: "Hey, Ayame! How's it going?"

Ayame: (faking a smile) "Oh, just enjoying the show. You were great out there."

Nobuhle notices the subtle sarcasm but brushes it off, thinking Ayame's just being friendly.

Nobuhle: "Thanks, it means a lot. This place... it's like a dream come true."

Ayame's smile fades for a second, her envy slipping through.

Ayame: (smirking) "Well, dreams have a way of... unraveling, don't they?"

Nobuhle frowns, sensing something off. Ayame shrugs and leaves the room, leaving Nobuhle slightly unsettled.

S cene 3: Planting Seeds of Doubt

The next day, Ayame is chatting with a few other musicians at the club, casually bringing up rumors to cast doubt on Nobuhle's reputation.

Ayame: "I mean, she's talented, no doubt. But I heard she didn't exactly have the cleanest past back in South Africa."

Musician 1: (curious) "Really? I hadn't heard that. She seems so... genuine."

Ayame: (pretending to hesitate) "Oh, I probably shouldn't say anything. Just... let's just say she might have been involved in some questionable things before she came here."

The musicians exchange uneasy glances, and Ayame smiles to herself, satisfied that the rumors have started to spread.

Scene 4: The Rumors Reach Nobuhle

A few days later, Nobuhle notices strange looks from her coworkers and overhears whispers as she walks past. Feeling unsettled, she approaches Hana, her friend, during a break.

Nobuhle: "Hana, has... has something been going around about me?"

Hana hesitates, glancing around before leaning closer.

Hana: "I wasn't going to say anything, but... yes. People are talking. They're saying you... you were involved in something illegal back in South Africa."

Nobuhle: (eyes widening) "What? That's not true! Who would say something like that?"

Hana gives her a sympathetic look.

Hana: "Ayame's been dropping hints. I don't know why, but... she seems to have it out for you."

Nobuhle clenches her fists, feeling both anger and fear. She's worked hard to start fresh, and now her past—whether true or not—is being used against her.

Scene 5: Confrontation

After her set that night, Nobuhle finds Ayame in the hallway outside the dressing room.

Nobuhle: (firmly) "Ayame, can we talk?"

Ayame raises an eyebrow, feigning innocence.

Ayame: "Sure, what's on your mind?"

Nobuhle: "I know you've been spreading rumors about me. Why? What did I do to you?"

Ayame lets out a small, dismissive laugh.

Ayame: "Oh, Nobuhle, don't be so sensitive. People talk. If you have nothing to hide, why are you so bothered?"

Nobuhle: (fuming) "Because you're trying to sabotage me! I came here to work, just like you. I don't understand why you're doing this."

Ayame crosses her arms, her face hardening.

Ayame: "You don't get it, do you? You think you can just walk in here and take what I've worked for? Tokyo doesn't need another starry-eyed singer trying to make it big. We're not all here to play fair."

Nobuhle clenches her jaw, refusing to back down.

Nobuhle: "I may not have been here as long as you, but I'm not going to let you tear me down with lies. I'll show everyone who I really am."

Ayame smirks, her confidence unwavering.

Ayame: "Good luck with that. People here believe what they want to believe. Let's see how long your little 'dream' lasts."

Nobuhle watches as Ayame saunters away, a mix of anger and determination rising within her. She knows she'll have to work even harder now to prove herself and regain the trust of her coworkers.

Scene 6: Support from Sibusiso

That night, Nobuhle meets with Sibusiso, her emotions bubbling over as she recounts what's happened.

Nobuhle: (frustrated) "She's trying to ruin everything, Sibu. I don't understand why she'd go this far."

Sibusiso listens, his face hardening as she explains Ayame's rumors.

Sibusiso: "People like that, they're scared. She probably sees how good you are, and it terrifies her."

Nobuhle sighs, looking down.

Nobuhle: "But what if people believe her? I came here to leave all of that behind, and now it's all catching up to me."

Sibusiso reaches across the table, gently squeezing her hand.

Sibusiso: "Then prove her wrong. Show them the real Nobuhle—the talented, hardworking musician who deserves to be here."

Nobuhle looks up, meeting his gaze, feeling a surge of confidence.

Nobuhle: "Thank you, Sibu. I don't know what I'd do without you."

They share a quiet moment, each finding strength in the other's support, resolved to face the challenges ahead together.

Chapter 9: Love in the Shadows

Scene 1: A Night Out

After a long week, Sibusiso and Nobuhle decide to spend the evening together, exploring Tokyo's vibrant nightlife. They stroll through the neon-lit streets of Shibuya, the air filled with laughter and the energy of the city.

Sibusiso: (smiling) "It's like the city never sleeps, isn't it? You can feel life all around you."

Nobuhle: (looking around, captivated) "It's... like being in a different world. Sometimes I can't believe I'm actually here."

They walk together in silence for a while, enjoying the moment, their hands brushing occasionally. Eventually, they find a small, cozy rooftop bar with a view of the Tokyo skyline and settle into a quiet corner, sipping drinks as they gaze out over the city.

Sibusiso: (softly) "I'm glad you're here with me, Nobuhle. I don't think I would've lasted this long without you."

Nobuhle: (smiling) "Same here. Somehow, you make this place feel a little more like home."

They sit close, shoulders touching. Their laughter fades into comfortable silence as they look out over the city, both feeling the weight of their shared history and new connection.

Scene 2: The First Kiss

Sibusiso turns to look at Nobuhle, his gaze lingering on her face. She senses it, looking back at him with a soft smile that slowly fades as she realizes the intensity of his gaze.

Nobuhle: (whispering) "Sibu..."

Sibusiso reaches up, gently brushing a stray strand of hair from her face. His hand lingers, and without thinking, he leans in, capturing her lips in a tender, hesitant kiss. Nobuhle melts into it, her hand resting lightly on his cheek.

They pull away slowly, both catching their breath, their foreheads resting together.

Sibusiso: (whispering) "I've been wanting to do that for so long."

Nobuhle: (smiling) "Me too."

They stay close, both feeling the depth of the moment but also sensing the unresolved tension that lies beneath the surface.

Scene 3: The Guilt Sets In

Back at his small apartment later that night, Sibusiso lies awake, staring at the ceiling, a mix of emotions swirling within him. The joy of finally connecting with Nobuhle in a way he's dreamed of is overshadowed by the guilt of hiding his past.

He sits up, rubbing his face, trying to shake off the unease. Flashbacks of the failed scams back in South Africa and the choices he made flood his mind.

Sibusiso: (to himself) "How can I expect her to trust me if I'm hiding who I really am?"

The thought gnaws at him. He knows that if he wants a real chance with Nobuhle, he'll have to come clean. But the fear of losing her is almost unbearable.

Scene 4: Nobuhle's Restlessness

Meanwhile, at her apartment, Nobuhle sits by the window, lost in thought. She replays the night over and over in her mind, feeling both exhilarated and uneasy. She, too, is haunted by the choices she made back in South Africa.

She picks up her phone, hesitating before sending Sibusiso a message.

Nobuhle: (texting) "Thank you for tonight. I haven't felt this way in a long time. Let's talk tomorrow?"

She stares at the screen, contemplating whether she, too, should tell him everything. A part of her worries he might see her differently if he knew the truth.

Nobuhle: (whispering) "I'm not ready to lose him... not yet."

Scene 5: Facing the Past

The next day, they meet for a quiet walk by the river. Sibusiso seems distracted, his face tense as they walk side by side.

Nobuhle: "You seem quiet today. Something on your mind?"

Sibusiso stops, looking out over the water before turning to her with a conflicted expression.

Sibusiso: "Nobuhle... there's something I need to tell you. About my past."

Nobuhle's heart skips a beat. She senses the seriousness in his tone and nods, bracing herself.

Nobuhle: "You can tell me anything, Sibu."

Sibusiso takes a deep breath, gathering his thoughts.

Sibusiso: "Back in South Africa, before I came here... I was involved in some things I'm not proud of. When everything fell apart during COVID, I made some mistakes. I tried... I tried to get quick money. It didn't work out, and I almost lost everything."

Nobuhle listens silently, her face softening as she sees the weight of his regret.

Nobuhle: "I understand, Sibu. You're not the only one who made mistakes."

Sibusiso looks at her, surprised.

Sibusiso: "You too?"

Nobuhle nods, taking his hand.

Nobuhle: "We both came here to start over, didn't we? Maybe it's time we let go of the guilt we've been carrying."

Sibusiso looks down, feeling a strange sense of relief mixed with vulnerability.

Sibusiso: "I was so scared to tell you. I thought... I thought you'd look at me differently."

Nobuhle: (smiling softly) "We all have shadows, Sibu. But we're here now, trying to be better. That's what matters."

They hold each other's hands tightly, both feeling a sense of hope, as if sharing their pasts has strengthened their bond.

Scene 6: A New Beginning

Later that evening, they sit by the water, watching the sunset. Nobuhle rests her head on Sibusiso's shoulder, feeling at peace for the first time in a long while.

Nobuhle: "I think we both needed this—someone who understands, who won't judge."

Sibusiso: "You're right. Maybe Tokyo was meant to be our second chance."

They share a quiet moment, their pasts no longer a burden between them. Both of them know they still have a long way to go, but now, they have each other to lean on.

Nobuhle: (smiling) "To new beginnings, then?"

Sibusiso: (holding her hand) "To new beginnings."

As the city lights begin to shimmer around them, they sit together in comfortable silence, feeling a profound connection that transcends their pasts.

Chapter 10: Kaito's Investigation

Scene 1: Kaito's Office

Detective Kaito Nakamura sits at his desk, sifting through recent case files. Photos of small-scale thefts, frauds, and minor scams involving foreigners are scattered before him. Leaning back, he sips his coffee and narrows his eyes at a report on Sibusiso.

Kaito: (thinking aloud) "South African...new in Tokyo...not much in terms of resources. He fits the profile."

He picks up a file and flips through it, intrigued by Sibusiso's background.

Kaito: "Mmm...only arrived a few months ago. Perhaps Tokyo wasn't his only escape."

He taps his fingers on the desk, contemplating his next move.

Kaito: "I'll need to get closer. A direct interrogation might make him shut down. But... a friend?"

Kaito's lips curve into a slight smile as he hatches his plan.

Scene 2: The First Meeting

Later that day, Kaito spots Sibusiso at a local café, scribbling in a notebook. Kaito approaches with a friendly demeanor, carrying his coffee and a small pastry.

Kaito: (smiling warmly) "Excuse me, are you from South Africa? I thought I overheard you speaking earlier."

Sibusiso looks up, surprised but nods politely.

Sibusiso: "Yes, that's right. I'm Sibusiso. And you are?"

Kaito: "Kaito Nakamura. I work...in public services here. I've always been fascinated by South African culture, though. Mind if I join?"

Sibusiso hesitates, sensing something odd about Kaito's approach, but eventually nods.

Sibusiso: "Sure, why not? Tokyo's an interesting place to have a fascination with South Africa."

Kaito: "Tokyo is a city of many interests. Sometimes, I meet people from different parts of the world, and each culture has its own stories. Speaking of, what brings you all the way here?"

Sibusiso shifts uncomfortably but keeps his answer vague.

Sibusiso: "Just a fresh start. I'm an author, so... thought I'd find some inspiration here."

Kaito: "An author, you say? Fascinating. There's so much to write about in Tokyo, especially with the mix of old and new."

They chat about South African and Japanese culture, and Sibusiso starts to feel a bit more at ease with Kaito.

Scene 3: Kaito's Suspicions Deepen

After a few more casual meetups, Kaito starts to gather subtle clues about Sibusiso's past. One evening, they walk through a quiet neighborhood after grabbing drinks, and Kaito subtly shifts the conversation to crime.

Kaito: "You know, Tokyo may seem peaceful, but we get our fair share of troublemakers here—some even from abroad. It's part of what I do, actually."

Sibusiso tenses slightly, hiding his reaction.

Sibusiso: "Oh really? I thought Japan was one of the safest countries."

Kaito: (nodding) "It is, but lately, we've had some... isolated incidents. Usually, it's just misunderstandings, foreigners not adapting to local ways."

He watches Sibusiso's reaction closely, noting a flash of guilt that quickly disappears.

Kaito: (smiling) "But I'm sure you're here just for your writing, right?"

Sibusiso: (forcing a chuckle) "Yeah, that's the plan. Just writing."

There's an awkward pause before Kaito shifts the conversation back to lighter topics, letting Sibusiso's guard drop once again.

Scene 4: Digging for Evidence

In his private moments, Kaito gathers more information about Sibusiso. He combs through surveillance footage, finding images of Sibusiso with Nobuhle and Jay, piecing together that their pasts may be more intertwined than Sibusiso has let on.

Kaito meets up with a fellow officer, Haruto, who assists him in his investigation.

Kaito: "I have a feeling he's hiding something, but I need more than a hunch. I'll keep him close, see if he slips up."

Haruto: "And the woman? Nobuhle, right? They seem close."

Kaito: "Yes, she could be key. I'll keep an eye on them both."

Scene 5: Another Friendly Meeting

Kaito and Sibusiso meet once again, this time at a park where Kaito subtly leads the conversation towards South African life.

Kaito: "You know, I read about South Africa's economic struggles. It must be hard to make ends meet."

Sibusiso nods, visibly uncomfortable with the topic.

Sibusiso: "Yeah, it's... challenging. But that's why I'm here, to start fresh."

Kaito: "Tokyo has its own set of challenges too, especially for newcomers. But I guess... we all have our own ways of getting by, right?"

Sibusiso picks up on the subtle implication, giving Kaito a wary look.

Sibusiso: "Right... though I prefer to keep things simple now. Just focusing on my work."

Kaito: (smiling) "That's admirable. But remember, if you ever need help adjusting, I'm here."

They shake hands, but as Sibusiso walks away, he senses something isn't quite right about Kaito's intentions.

Scene 6: Doubts and Paranoia

Back at his apartment, Sibusiso replays the interactions in his mind, feeling a creeping sense of paranoia. Nobuhle calls, and he hesitates but eventually answers.

Nobuhle: "Hey, Sibu. How was your day?"

Sibusiso: "Fine... just, I've been spending time with this guy, Kaito. He seems friendly, but I can't shake the feeling he knows more than he lets on."

Nobuhle: "Maybe he's just curious. It's not every day he meets a South African writer."

Sibusiso: (sighing) "I don't know... I just need to be careful. We came here to escape that life, remember?"

Nobuhle: "Yes, and we're doing that. But if this Kaito guy is making you uncomfortable, maybe distance yourself a bit."

Sibusiso: "Yeah... maybe."

As they end the call, Sibusiso knows he'll need to be cautious around Kaito, who, he suspects, may have a hidden agenda.

Chapter 11: The Unraveling

Scene 1: The Breaking News

It's a typical evening at the jazz club. Nobuhle just wrapped up her set, basking in the applause. As she steps off the stage, she notices her phone lighting up with endless notifications. Puzzled, she checks it and finds dozens of messages and missed calls.

Nobuhle: (whispering to herself) "What on earth...?"

She opens a message from Hana, reading the headline: **"Scandal Unveiled: Rising Jazz Star's Criminal Past Revealed."** *Nobuhle's heart sinks, and her hands begin to shake. She rushes out the back door to find some air.*

Scene 2: Sibusiso's Discovery

Meanwhile, Sibusiso is working at a small cafe when his phone buzzes with a news alert. He clicks it, only to see Nobuhle's face plastered across the screen with bold accusations about her past.

Sibusiso: (under his breath) "No... No, this can't be happening."

He grabs his things and races to the jazz club, panic overtaking him.

Scene 3: Confrontation Outside the Jazz Club

Outside the club, Nobuhle paces in a panic, her face pale. She barely notices Sibusiso running up to her.

Sibusiso: "Nobuhle!"

Nobuhle turns, her eyes wide with fear and anger.

Nobuhle: "They found out, Sibu. Someone leaked everything."

Sibusiso: (placing a hand on her shoulder) "We'll figure this out. Do you have any idea who could've done this?"

Nobuhle: (thinking, then her face hardens) "Ayame. It has to be her. She's been looking for any excuse to ruin me."

Sibusiso sighs, anger simmering beneath his calm exterior.

Sibusiso: "Of course it's her. But don't worry, we'll handle it. Let's get out of here for now."

Nobuhle hesitates but finally nods, letting him lead her down the street away from the club.

Scene 4: The Safe House

They reach Sibusiso's small apartment, and Nobuhle collapses onto the couch, visibly shaken. Sibusiso brings her a glass of water.

Sibusiso: "Hey, you're safe here. Let's just think things through. We can make a plan."

Nobuhle: "I don't even know what to do. I was finally getting somewhere... and now it feels like everything's falling apart."

Sibusiso: "You're stronger than this. You've come this far, right? And you don't have to face it alone."

They share a long look, a silent understanding passing between them. But Sibusiso's expression grows tense.

Sibusiso: "Nobuhle, there's something I need to tell you."

Nobuhle: (raising an eyebrow) "What is it?"

Sibusiso: (taking a deep breath) "You're not the only one with secrets."

Nobuhle stares at him, her brows furrowing in confusion.

Nobuhle: "What are you saying, Sibu?"

Sibusiso: "I have a past too, Nobuhle. Back in South Africa... I wasn't exactly on the right side of the law."

He hesitates, watching her reaction.

Nobuhle: (stunned) "Are you telling me... you were involved in crime too?"

Sibusiso: (nodding) "Yes. I did things I'm not proud of. But I left that life behind to be here, to start over."

Nobuhle: (exhaling slowly) "Sibu, why didn't you tell me this before?"

Sibusiso: "Because I thought I could escape it. But seeing what's happening to you, it's made me realize we can't keep running from our pasts forever."

Nobuhle is silent for a moment, absorbing his confession.

Nobuhle: "So... what do we do now?"

Sibusiso: "We fight back. We show everyone that we're more than our mistakes."

Nobuhle nods, a new resolve in her eyes.

Nobuhle: "Alright. Let's do it. Together."

Scene 5: The Fallout and the Plan

Over the next few days, Nobuhle and Sibusiso face a whirlwind of backlash. Nobuhle loses gigs at the jazz club, and her social media is flooded with hurtful messages. Yet she finds strength in Sibusiso, who stands by her side through the storm.

Sibusiso: "If Ayame thinks she's going to get away with this, she's got another thing coming."

Nobuhle: "She doesn't know who she's dealing with."

They start plotting their next moves, determined to prove they're more than their pasts.

Scene 6: Unveiling Their True Selves

They set up a press conference, inviting media and supporters to hear their side of the story. Nobuhle stands in front of a small crowd, Sibusiso beside her.

Nobuhle: (clearing her throat) "I made mistakes in my past. I'm not proud of them, but they don't define who I am today."

The crowd murmurs, and Nobuhle catches Sibusiso's encouraging nod.

Nobuhle: "I came to Tokyo to find a new beginning, to start fresh and prove to myself that I could make something of my life."

Sibusiso takes over, addressing the audience.

Sibusiso: "We both came here carrying the weight of our pasts, hoping to escape them. But Tokyo has shown us that we can't run forever."

Nobuhle nods in agreement, her voice strong.

Nobuhle: "I'm not hiding anymore. I'm ready to face whatever comes my way, and I hope you'll judge me by who I am now, not who I once was."

Scene 7: The Aftermath

The press conference stirs up mixed reactions. Some are sympathetic, while others remain skeptical. Yet, both Sibusiso and Nobuhle feel a sense of freedom in being open.

Sibusiso: (smiling at Nobuhle) "We did it. We faced them."

Nobuhle: "And we survived. Whatever happens next, at least we've got each other."

They walk out of the press room hand in hand, ready to take on whatever challenges lie ahead.

Chapter 12: Confronting the Past

Scene 1: The Confession

Sibusiso and Nobuhle are sitting in Sibusiso's dimly lit apartment. The weight of their secrets presses on both of them, creating an uneasy silence.

Sibusiso: (hesitantly) "Nobuhle, there's more I haven't told you."

Nobuhle turns to him, her expression a mix of curiosity and worry.

Nobuhle: "What do you mean? I thought you already told me everything."

Sibusiso lowers his head, struggling to find the right words.

Sibusiso: "No, not everything. I... I tried to do something, back in South Africa, when things got really bad."

Nobuhle's eyes narrow slightly, sensing the gravity of what he's about to reveal.

Nobuhle: "What did you do, Sibu?"

Sibusiso: (sighing deeply) "When I lost my job, and I was completely broke, I tried... well, let's just say I tried to make quick money in ways I'm not proud of. But each attempt went wrong, and I almost got caught. Eventually, I knew I had to leave South Africa before things spiraled out of control."

Nobuhle's expression turns from concern to something colder, harder to read.

Nobuhle: "You mean... you tried to commit crimes? You never told me any of this."

Sibusiso: (nodding slowly) "I didn't want to burden you with it. I thought it was something I could bury in the past, but now I see that hiding it from you was a mistake."

Nobuhle: (pulling away slightly) "A mistake? You lied to me, Sibu. You made me believe we were in this together, that we'd left our pasts behind."

Sibusiso looks at her, his expression filled with regret.

Sibusiso: "I know, and I'm sorry. I thought I was protecting you, but I see now that I was only protecting myself from facing what I did."

Nobuhle: "Do you know how hard it was for me to trust you? To let you in after everything I went through?"

Sibusiso reaches out, but Nobuhle pulls back, her face a mixture of hurt and anger.

Sibusiso: "I understand if you're angry. I just want you to know I'm not that person anymore. I came here to start fresh, just like you did."

Nobuhle: "And yet, here we are, with both of our pasts staring us in the face. Maybe we were foolish to think we could escape it."

Scene 2: The Distance Between Them

Days pass, and an uncomfortable distance grows between them. Nobuhle spends more time at the jazz club, avoiding Sibusiso. He, in turn, throws himself into his writing, trying to drown out his guilt.

Nobuhle is at the club, confiding in Mika, her mentor, over a quiet cup of tea.

Mika: "You seem troubled, Nobuhle. Is it about that news story?"

Nobuhle: (shaking her head) "No... well, yes, but it's more than that. Sibusiso... he lied to me. He kept parts of his past hidden, and I feel like I barely know him now."

Mika: "Ah, the secrets of the heart can be heavy burdens. But are you certain that his intentions were wrong?"

Nobuhle: (sighing) "I just feel like everything's slipping through my fingers. I'm trying so hard to build a life here, and yet I can't help feeling trapped by what we left behind."

Mika: "Sometimes, the only way forward is through the truth, even if it hurts."

Nobuhle nods, contemplating Mika's words, though a shadow of doubt lingers.

Scene 3: The Confrontation

That evening, Sibusiso waits outside the jazz club, hoping to catch Nobuhle on her way out. She steps outside, surprised to see him there.

Sibusiso: "Nobuhle, please. Can we talk?"

Nobuhle: (crossing her arms) "What is there to talk about? You lied, Sibu. You kept me in the dark."

Sibusiso: "I didn't want to, but I was ashamed. I thought if I could just move past it, we'd be okay."

Nobuhle: "But we're not okay. Don't you see that? We're carrying our pasts around like shadows, and every time we think we're free, they drag us back."

Sibusiso: (lowering his voice) "Maybe you're right. But we've both made mistakes. I just want to be honest with you now. Whatever happens, I don't want to lose you, Nobuhle."

Nobuhle: "How can I believe that? Every time I try to trust you, there's something else hidden beneath the surface."

Sibusiso steps closer, his voice filled with emotion.

Sibusiso: "Because I'm here now, telling you everything. I don't want to hide anymore, Nobuhle. I want to face this with you, whatever that means."

She looks at him, her gaze softening for a moment before hardening again.

Nobuhle: "I just need some time, Sibu. I need to figure out if I can really do this... if we can really make this work."

Sibusiso nods, his face a mixture of understanding and sadness.

Sibusiso: "I understand. Take all the time you need."

Nobuhle turns and walks away, leaving Sibusiso standing alone under the dim streetlights.

Scene 4: Reflection

In the following days, both Sibusiso and Nobuhle grapple with their inner conflicts. Sibusiso writes furiously, pouring his regret and longing onto the page. Nobuhle, meanwhile, confides in Hana, whose blunt honesty stirs something within her.

Hana: "So, you're telling me he made mistakes? Welcome to humanity."

Nobuhle: "It's more than that, Hana. It's the lies, the secrecy... I don't know if I can handle it."

Hana: "Everyone's carrying something, Nobuhle. Maybe it's about deciding what's worth fighting for. Or who."

Nobuhle considers this, and a flicker of hope begins to take root.

Scene 5: A Moment of Clarity

One evening, Sibusiso sits in his apartment, scrolling through old photos on his phone. He stops at one of him and Nobuhle, smiling brightly at each other during better times. He stares at it for a long moment before dialing her number.

Sibusiso: (on the phone) "Nobuhle... I know you need space, but I just wanted to tell you that I'm here. Whenever you're ready to talk, I'll be here."

Nobuhle: (pausing) "Thank you, Sibu."

Scene 6: The Decision

A few days later, Nobuhle finds herself outside Sibusiso's apartment. She takes a deep breath and knocks on the door.

He opens it, his expression a mixture of surprise and hope.

Nobuhle: "I've been thinking. Maybe we both have things we're ashamed of, things we wish we could change. But... I don't want to keep running."

Sibusiso: (hopeful) "So what does that mean?"

Nobuhle: (smiling slightly) "It means that if we're going to do this, we have to do it right. No more secrets, no more hiding."

Sibusiso nods, relief washing over him.

Sibusiso: "Agreed. No more secrets."

They share a look of mutual understanding, both realizing that their love might just be strong enough to withstand the weight of their pasts.

Chapter 13: Crossroads of Desperation

Scene 1: The Proposition

Sibusiso is in his apartment, pacing back and forth. The rent is due, his literary prospects are dwindling, and the pressure mounts as he thinks about Jay's offer. He pulls out his phone, staring at Jay's number.

Sibusiso: (muttering to himself) "This isn't what I came here for. But maybe... just one time."

His phone rings suddenly, and he sees Jay's name on the screen. He hesitates before answering.

Jay: "Hey, Sibu! Thought you'd gone quiet on me. You still thinking about my offer?"

Sibusiso: (pausing) "Yeah... I am. Things are tight, Jay. Real tight."

Jay: (with a sly tone) "I told you, man, it's easy cash. One job, and you're set for a few months. We know how to play it smart."

Sibusiso: (hesitantly) "But it's risky. What if it backfires?"

Jay: "Come on, Sibu. Since when did you become scared of taking chances? Think about it. You're talented, but talent needs cash to breathe. You want to live on dreams or get things done?"

Sibusiso sighs, torn between his principles and his growing desperation.

Sibusiso: "Give me a little more time to think, Jay. I'll get back to you."

He hangs up, visibly conflicted.

Scene 2: Nobuhle's Doubts

At the jazz club, Nobuhle is sitting at a dimly lit table, staring out at the stage where she usually performs. Mika joins her, setting a cup of tea down in front of her.

Mika: "You look like you're carrying the world on your shoulders, Nobuhle."

Nobuhle: (sighing) "It's just... everything feels so hard right now. The rumors, the scrutiny, and the feeling that I'm constantly fighting just to belong here."

Mika: (nodding thoughtfully) "Sometimes, the things worth having demand the most of us. You have talent, Nobuhle. Don't let anyone scare you out of what you're building here."

Nobuhle: "But at what cost, Mika? I feel like I'm losing myself. Every day is a battle to prove that I belong. Maybe it's time to accept that Tokyo isn't the place for me."

Mika: (leaning forward) "You've come too far to let fear make your decisions. You're stronger than that. And remember, the world will always doubt us, but we're the ones who decide when we leave."

Nobuhle: (quietly) "I don't even know if staying is worth the emotional toll. It's exhausting, always looking over my shoulder, always questioning myself."

Mika: "Only you can answer that, Nobuhle. But whatever choice you make, make sure it's for you, not because others pushed you into it."

Nobuhle looks down, reflecting on Mika's words, feeling both comforted and challenged.

Scene 3: A Brief Meeting

Later that evening, Sibusiso and Nobuhle meet at a small café, their faces both tense. The strain is visible as they sit across from each other, nursing their drinks.

Nobuhle: "Sibu, have you thought about... maybe going back home?"

Sibusiso: (surprised) "Going back? I came here for a fresh start, Nobuhle. I don't want to go back just because things got tough."

Nobuhle: "I know, but sometimes I feel like this city is swallowing me whole. And with everything that's been happening... I'm honestly considering it."

Sibusiso: (after a pause) "I get it. Tokyo's not what we expected. But maybe this is part of the test—to see if we're strong enough to stick it out."

Nobuhle sighs, looking away as a wave of doubt crosses her face.

Nobuhle: "What if we're just fooling ourselves? We came here to escape, but our pasts followed us. Maybe it's a sign."

Sibusiso: (with a small, rueful smile) "Funny, I was thinking the same thing. I got a... proposal, from someone I knew back home. It's not exactly the kind of thing I want to get into, but..."

Nobuhle: "Sibu, no. You can't go back to that life."

Sibusiso: "And you think I don't know that? But I'm barely holding on here. And sometimes... sometimes it feels like the only choice left."

Scene 4: A Moment of Reconsideration

The next day, Nobuhle stands backstage at the jazz club, about to perform. She watches the crowd, feeling the weight of the rumors and whispers. Mika approaches, sensing her apprehension.

Mika: "You have a choice, Nobuhle. You can let their whispers define you, or you can rise above it. Show them why you're here."

Nobuhle takes a deep breath, feeling a renewed determination as she steps out on stage.

Nobuhle: (to herself) "This is for me."

Her performance is raw, heartfelt, as she channels her frustrations and dreams into every note. The crowd is captivated, their previous judgments forgotten, at least for the moment.

Scene 5: A Turning Point

After the performance, Nobuhle finds herself in the empty club, reflecting on her decision to stay. Sibusiso arrives, his expression contemplative.

Sibusiso: "I saw your performance. You were... incredible."

Nobuhle: "Thank you. I needed that reminder of why I'm here."

Sibusiso: (taking a deep breath) "I made a decision too. I'm not going to take Jay's offer. Whatever happens, I'm not going down that road again."

Nobuhle: (relieved) "Thank you, Sibu. I don't want either of us to lose sight of who we're trying to become here."

Sibusiso nods, the weight of their conversation lifting slightly as they sit together in the quiet of the empty club, both feeling a newfound sense of clarity.

Chapter 14: A Second Chance

Scene 1: Nobuhle's Resolve

It's early morning, and Nobuhle is standing by her window, watching the Tokyo skyline as the city awakens. She feels a newfound determination surging within her.

Nobuhle: (murmuring to herself) "This is my life. I'm not going to let anyone take that from me."

She heads to the jazz club with a confident stride, rehearsing in her mind how she'll face the club manager, Mika, and her colleagues.

At the club, she finds Mika busy reviewing the lineup for the night. Nobuhle approaches her, her voice steady.

Nobuhle: "Mika, I want to talk to you."

Mika: (looking up, surprised) "Nobuhle. I wasn't sure if you'd come back after everything that's happened."

Nobuhle: "I know I have a lot to prove, and I'm willing to work as hard as it takes to repair my reputation. I'm not here to run away anymore."

Mika watches her, noting the new determination in her eyes.

Mika: "This industry can be unforgiving. You'll need to be stronger than you've ever been, and stay focused."

Nobuhle: "I understand. And I'm ready. If you'll let me, I want to keep performing here."

Mika nods slowly, a hint of approval in her gaze.

Mika: "Alright, Nobuhle. Let's see what you're made of."

Nobuhle smiles, feeling the weight of her decision lift slightly. This is her chance to reclaim her place in Tokyo.

Scene 2: Sibusiso's Liberation

Meanwhile, Sibusiso meets Jay at a café. Jay is casually seated, exuding his usual confidence, but Sibusiso has made up his mind.

Jay: (grinning) "I knew you'd come around, Sibu. Let's talk business."

Sibusiso: (shaking his head) "Jay, I didn't come here to accept. I'm done. Whatever you're planning—I'm out."

Jay: (surprised) "What? You're going to walk away from easy money? Do you know how hard it is to make it here?"

***Sibusiso:** "Yeah, I do. And I also know that if I go down this path again, I'll never forgive myself. This city offered me a second chance, and I'm not going to waste it."

Jay: (scoffing) "You're letting pride get in the way. This is Tokyo—nobody survives here on principles."

Sibusiso: "Maybe. But I'd rather struggle on my own terms than get dragged back into the life I left behind."

Jay stares at him, trying to read his resolve.

Jay: "Fine, Sibu. Go play the starving artist if that's what you want. But don't come crying to me when you're broke."

Sibusiso stands, feeling the weight lift as he walks away, leaving Jay behind for good.

Scene 3: Turning Experiences into Art

Later that day, Sibusiso meets Yuto at a local bookstore café. Yuto is reading through some pages of Sibusiso's draft.

Yuto: "This is good, Sibusiso. But it feels like you're holding back."

Sibusiso: (sighing) "There's a lot I'm not sure about yet. I want to write honestly, but my past... it's messy."

Yuto: "Use it. People connect with authenticity, not perfection. Don't hide what you've been through. That's where the real story is."

Sibusiso: "You think people would want to read that? About the struggles, the mistakes?"

Yuto: "Absolutely. Look around—Tokyo is full of people trying to escape something. Show them that change is possible."

Sibusiso nods, feeling a renewed sense of purpose. His story has value, and maybe, sharing it could be his way to finally reconcile with his past.

Scene 4: Nobuhle's Return to the Stage

That evening, Nobuhle stands backstage at the jazz club, nervously adjusting her dress as she prepares for her performance. The club is packed, and she feels the pressure mounting, but she reminds herself of why she's there.

Mika approaches her, offering a reassuring smile.

Mika: "Remember, Nobuhle, this is your moment. Own it."

Nobuhle takes a deep breath, nodding before stepping out onto the stage. The crowd falls silent as she picks up the microphone, her gaze sweeping over the audience. She closes her eyes and begins to sing, pouring her heart into each note.

Her performance is raw, vulnerable, and hauntingly beautiful. By the time she finishes, the audience is captivated, and applause erupts, louder than she's ever heard before.

Nobuhle smiles, feeling a deep sense of accomplishment. She's proven to herself and to everyone that she belongs here.

Scene 5: Sibusiso's Breakthrough

A few days later, Sibusiso completes a rough draft of his manuscript, feeling both nervous and exhilarated. He meets Yuto at the café to share the finished work.

Sibusiso: (handing over the manuscript) "It's all there. The truth, the struggles... everything."

Yuto: (flipping through the pages) "This is powerful, Sibusiso. It's not just a story—it's a journey. You've captured something real."

Sibusiso: "I never thought I'd get here. I owe a lot to this city... and to the people who believed in me."

Yuto smiles, placing a reassuring hand on Sibusiso's shoulder.

Yuto: "Tokyo gave you a second chance, and you took it. That's something to be proud of."

Scene 6: Reconciliation

One evening, Nobuhle and Sibusiso meet at the jazz club after her performance. They sit together, a comfortable silence settling between them.

Nobuhle: (smiling) "Feels like things are finally coming together."

Sibusiso: "Yeah. We've both been through a lot to get here, but I think it was worth it."

Nobuhle: "I've been thinking... maybe we don't need to run from our pasts anymore. Maybe it's time to accept who we were and focus on who we're becoming."

Sibusiso: "I think you're right. Tokyo has its way of making us face our truths. I've learned that honesty—especially with ourselves—is the only way forward."

They share a meaningful look, realizing how much they've grown individually and together.

Scene 7: Embracing the Future

A few weeks later, Sibusiso's book is accepted by a publishing house, and Nobuhle's performances gain a loyal following at the club. They celebrate together, feeling a newfound sense of peace and accomplishment.

Sibusiso: "To new beginnings and second chances."

Nobuhle: (raising her glass) "And to letting go of the past."

They clink glasses, their faces reflecting a sense of pride and contentment as they look toward the future, ready to embrace whatever comes next.

Chapter 15: Lost and Found

Scene 1: An Unexpected Meeting

Sibusiso sits at a small café in Shibuya, staring out the window at the bustling street. His laptop is open, but his mind wanders. Suddenly, he hears a familiar voice behind him.

Nobuhle: (teasing) "Still brooding over a blank page, Sibu?"

Sibusiso turns, surprised to see Nobuhle standing there, smiling shyly. She's carrying her guitar case and looks radiant, her confidence back.

Sibusiso: (grinning) "Well, well, look who decided to grace me with her presence. How did you find me?"

Nobuhle: "Tokyo's big, but not that big. You always said you loved this spot."

She sits across from him, placing her guitar case beside her. For a moment, they just look at each other, the weight of their shared history hanging in the air.

Nobuhle: (softly) "I missed you, Sibusiso."

Sibusiso: "I missed you too, Buhle. More than you know."

Scene 2: A Shared Confession

Later, they walk through Yoyogi Park, the autumn leaves creating a kaleidoscope of red and gold around them. Sibusiso hesitates, then speaks.

Sibusiso: "I've been thinking about everything. About us. About the mess we've been through."

Nobuhle: "Me too. I kept running away from my past, thinking I could leave it behind, but... it's a part of me. I can't erase it."

Sibusiso: "Neither can I. But maybe we don't have to. Maybe we can take everything we've learned, everything we've been through, and build something new. Together."

Nobuhle: (stopping to look at him) "Do you mean that?"

Sibusiso: "Every word."

Scene 3: Supporting Each Other's Dreams

Over the next few weeks, Nobuhle and Sibusiso begin to rebuild their lives, this time together. Sibusiso finishes his manuscript and sends it to Yuto, who calls him the next day.

Yuto: (on the phone) "This is incredible, Sibusiso. Raw, honest, and real. This is the kind of story people need right now."

Sibusiso: "Thanks, Yuto. I couldn't have done it without Nobuhle. She's been my anchor through all of this."

Meanwhile, Nobuhle performs her original songs at the jazz club, drawing bigger crowds each night. After one particularly electrifying performance, Mika pulls her aside.

Mika: "Nobuhle, you've found your voice. You're not just singing anymore—you're telling your story."

Nobuhle: "That's because I finally believe in it. Thank you, Mika, for giving me the chance."

Scene 4: Facing the Past Together

One evening, Sibusiso and Nobuhle sit on the rooftop of his apartment building, overlooking Tokyo's neon-lit skyline. Sibusiso places a hand over hers.

Sibusiso: "You know, there's one thing we haven't done yet. We haven't really confronted our pasts."

Nobuhle: "You're right. But I don't think we have to do it alone anymore."

Sibusiso: "No. We don't."

They share a quiet moment, the weight of their pasts finally feeling lighter.

Scene 5: A Future on Their Terms

Months later, Nobuhle's music is gaining traction, and Sibusiso's book is published to critical acclaim. They stand together at her album release party, surrounded by friends and supporters.

Nobuhle: (smiling at Sibusiso) "You know, I used to think Tokyo was just a place to escape to. But now I realize it's where I found myself."

Sibusiso: "And where I found you."

They share a tender kiss, the noise of the party fading around them. For the first time in their lives, they feel at peace—not because their struggles are over, but because they've learned to face them together.

Scene 6: A Final Reflection

The next day, they walk through a quiet temple garden. Nobuhle carries her guitar, and Sibusiso has his notebook tucked under his arm.

Nobuhle: "Do you ever think about going back to South Africa?"

Sibusiso: "Sometimes. But not yet. Tokyo still has a few more stories for us, I think."

Nobuhle: "Maybe. But wherever we go next, we'll go together."

Sibusiso smiles, taking her hand as they continue down the path, the future stretching out before them like a blank page, ready to be filled.

End of Chapter 15

Book Description

Amid the neon-lit streets and serene temples of Tokyo, two South African dreamers, Sibusiso and Nobuhle, find themselves worlds away from home—and from the lives they once knew.

Sibusiso, an aspiring author, and Nobuhle, a musician with a voice as soulful as her spirit, are united by shared struggles and a burning desire to rebuild their lives. After losing everything in South Africa during the COVID-19 pandemic, they arrive in Tokyo, each chasing a fresh start. But the shadows of their past threaten to catch up with them, and their paths cross in ways they never expected.

While Sibusiso battles inner demons and temptations from an old accomplice, Nobuhle faces fierce rivalries and rumors in the city's vibrant jazz scene. As they navigate the pressures of ambition, the allure of forbidden shortcuts, and the weight of their secrets, they find solace in each other.

But when the truth about their pasts is revealed, will their love survive the fallout?

Lost in Tokyo, Found in You is a poignant and dramatic tale of resilience, redemption, and the transformative power of love in the most unexpected places. For anyone who's ever lost their way, this is a story of finding yourself—and the person you're meant to be with.

Don't miss out!

Visit the website below and you can sign up to receive emails whenever Sibusiso Anthon Mkhwanazi publishes a new book. There's no charge and no obligation.

https://books2read.com/r/B-A-QNVAB-YCLKF

BOOKS2READ

Connecting independent readers to independent writers.

Did you love *Lost in Tokyo found in you*? Then you should read *Connected Hearts*[1] by Sibusiso Anthon Mkhwanazi!

In a world where love often feels out of reach, Sibusiso and Nombuso find each other in the unlikeliest place—a TikTok live session. What begins as a simple conversation quickly blossoms into a connection neither of them expected. Separated by miles, with Sibusiso in Johannesburg and Nombuso in Durban, they embark on a journey of love, trust, and determination to overcome the challenges of a long-distance relationship.From nervous first meetings to intimate moments that deepen their bond, their story captures the beauty and vulnerability of two souls finding home in each other. As they

---

1. https://books2read.com/u/md9Qx5

2. https://books2read.com/u/md9Qx5

navigate the complexities of their connection, their shared dreams and unwavering commitment remind us that love truly knows no bounds.Connected Hearts: A TikTok Love Story is a modern romance about the power of connection, the courage to take a chance, and the magic of finding love when you least expect it.

Also by Sibusiso Anthon Mkhwanazi

Million-Dollar Decade

Resilience Beyond Pain

Resonance Of Hope

Cheating hearts to true love

The Dream Builders Of Daveyton

Before the Bible

Ink and Imagination

Becoming A Millionaire In South Africa

Leaders of the World

Mining In Africa

Origins of Language and Civilization

Vita Nova Centre

Sisters of A cursed bloodline

Witchcraft in Africa

Ghosts of the golden city

Connected Hearts

Lost in Tokyo found in you

About the Author

Sibusiso Anthon Mkhwanazi is a versatile and dynamic author from Daveyton, South Africa. Known for his ability to navigate multiple genres with ease, his writing captures the complexities of human experiences, blending heartfelt emotion, gripping narratives, and vivid storytelling.

Sibusiso's work spans crime fiction, romance, poetry, and motivational writing. He is the creative force behind several upcoming books, including Sisters of a Cursed Bloodline, Under the Roof There is No Money: A Millionaire's Journey, and Shuffle: The Rise of Kabelo Dlamini. His stories often explore themes of resilience, love, family dynamics, and the pursuit of success, resonating deeply with readers.

Inspired by his own journey, Sibusiso also writes about the challenges and triumphs of life in South Africa. From tales of hardship to uplifting narratives of self-made success, his work reflects the vibrancy and struggles of his community. His romance novel Lost in Tokyo, Found in You beautifully weaves love and adventure, set against the backdrop of one of the world's most iconic cities.

Sibusiso's passion for storytelling began in his youth and has blossomed into a career as a multi-genre author. When he's not writing, he works as a cleaner for Tsebo Cleaning Solutions at Botshelong Hospital, drawing inspiration from the resilience of everyday people.

Through his diverse projects, Sibusiso Anthon Mkhwanazi is fast becoming a compelling voice in South African literature, committed to creating stories that entertain, inspire, and empower.